Zug and the Little Blue Tug

Colin and Jacqui Hawkins

FAMILY LEARNING

It's a lovely day to sail away!

FAMILY LEARNING

from Dorling Kindersley

The Family Learning mission is to support the concept of the home as a center of learning and to help families develop independent learning skills to last a lifetime.

Editors: Bridget Gibbs, Fiona Munro, Constance Robinson
Designers: Chris Fraser, Lisa Hollis

Published by Family Learning

Southland Executive Park, 7800 Southland Boulevard
Orlando, Florida 32809

Dorling Kindersley registered offices:
9 Henrietta Street, Covent Garden, London WC2E 8PS

VISIT US ON THE WORLD WIDE WEB AT:
www.dk.com

ISBN 0-7894-4676-6

Color reproduction by DOT Gradations
Printed in Hong Kong by Wing King Tong

Have you heard of Zug?
He's the bug who lives on a tug.
"I'm the bug with the tug!" said Zug.

Inside the tug, it was warm and snug, with a cozy stove and woolly rug. At night to rest his sleepy head, Zug slept in a little bunk bed.

When it was dark
and stormy outside,
Zug was safe and warm inside.
"I'm snug as a bug in a tug!"
laughed Zug as he drank
hot chocolate from his mug.
"Chug! Chug!" went Tug.

He polished Tug every day
to keep the salt and rust away.
"I like this color, do you?" said Zug,
as he painted Tug a bright sea blue.
"Chug! Chug!" chugged Tug.

The little blue tug was very strong from tugging barges all day long. Up the river and out to sea, the two were busy as could be.

"I'm the captain of the best tug afloat," said Zug the bug to the little tugboat. "Chug! Chug!" went Tug.

One day Zug tied up the tug and
went to meet his Ladybug.
"I've got a date – but I
won't be late," said Zug
the bug to the little tug.

"I'm in love, give me a hug,"
said Zug to Ladybug.
But Ladybug gave a shrug,
and said, "You're such a
creepy-crawly, Zug.
You're always on that tug at sea
and never come and visit me."

"Forget about that Ladybug," said Zug's friend, Pug. "There's no point in wishing. Let's go fishing."
"It's a deal. I'll get my rod and reel," said Zug.

"This is a hoot," said Zug to Pug,
as he caught an old boot, then lots of pans,
old tin cans, a rusty
bike, and a
grumpy
pike!

Suddenly, a
huge boat shot past,
going very, very fast.
On board was Mig the
superstar pig – the pig in
the wig who had made it big.
"Out of the way, little tug!"
shouted Mig to Zug and Pug.
"Stay afloat, little boat!" said Zug.
"Glug! Glug!" glugged Tug.

Pug and Zug were quite upset.
The waves had made them very
wet. As Mig's boat sailed on
across the sea, Zug shouted,
"I'm soaked, just look at me!"
"And me!" said Pug.

Zug was not a happy bug.
"Let's head for home," he said to Pug.
"We couldn't be wetter," Pug said to Zug,
"but a mug of cocoa will make us feel better."
Suddenly, over the radio came an S.O.S.
Who was it from? Can you guess?

"Hello, hello, can you hear me, Zug?
I'm sorry I splashed you
and your friend Pug.
I need help to get afloat,
I need a tug from the
little tugboat,"
said Mig to Zug.

Mig's boat was in big trouble.
She needed help on the double.
She had at last run out of luck
and on a sandbank
she was stuck.

To Mig's boat Zug hooked a chain, and then
Tug began to strain. Tug tugged and
chugged, and chugged and tugged.
"You can do it," said Zug.
"Come on, Tug," said Pug.
Then with one last mighty lug,
Tug pulled Mig's boat free,
and off it floated on the sea.
Yippee!

Toward home was Mig's boat tugged by Tug.
"Well done, Tug!" said Zug and Pug.
The little tug felt
very proud with
all the cheers
from the crowd.

Mig kissed Zug, then kissed Pug,
then gave Tug a great big hug.
"I love you guys,
you deserve a prize!
Would you like to go
on my big TV show?"
"Chug! Chug!" chugged Tug.

"I don't love Ladybug
any more. It's Mig the pig
I adore," said Zug.
"Chug! Chug!" chugged Tug.